ma[...] [...]ley

TWO of a kind ™

War [...] he Wardrobes

Look for these

titles:

mary-kateandashley

TWO of a kind ™

War of the Wardrobes

by Megan Stine

from the series created by Robert Griffard
& Howard Adler

HarperCollins*Entertainment*
An Imprint of HarperCollins*Publishers*

A PARACHUTE PRESS BOOK

A PARACHUTE PRESS BOOK
Parachute Publishing, L.L.C.
156 Fifth Avenue
Suite 325
NEW YORK
NY 10010

First published in the USA by HarperEntertainment 2000
First published in Great Britain by HarperCollins*Entertainment* 2003
HarperCollins*Entertainment* is an imprint of HarperCollins*Publishers* Ltd,
77-85 Fulham Palace Road, Hammersmith, London W6 8JB

The HarperCollins website address is
www.**fire**and**water**.com

1 3 5 7 9 8 6 4 2

The authors assert the moral right to be
identified as the authors of the work.

ISBN 0 00 714468 7

Printed and bound in Great Britain by Clays Ltd, St Ives plc

CHAPTER ONE

"Say it's not true," Ashley Burke begged her friend Wendy. "Please – tell me it's a joke. Just a cruel, ugly joke. We *can't* be getting school uniforms!"

Wendy Linden shook her head. "It's no joke. Everyone at White Oak Academy will be wearing uniforms by the end of the month. My mom said so."

Ashley rolled her eyes and glanced at her friends. She and her twin sister, Mary-Kate, were hanging out in the lounge of Porter House, their dorm at boarding school.

"But how can you be sure?" Elise Van Hook asked. "Maybe it's just a rumour."

1

Ashley remembered that Elise was new at White Oak. She didn't always have the inside scoop.

"Wendy's mom is on the board of trustees," Ashley explained. "If anyone would know, she would."

"It's not fair," Samantha Kramer said. "I just bought a whole new wardrobe for this term!"

"Me, too," Ashley agreed. "I've been waiting three weeks for it to be cold enough to wear my new ski-sweater outfit."

"Well, you'd better wear it soon," Wendy advised. "The board of trustees is going to decide about the uniforms during Homecoming Weekend. That's only two weeks away."

"Homecoming?" Elise's eyes lit up. "Does that mean we get to have a big dance – and elect a queen?"

"Not us," Mary-Kate said, shaking her head. "The girls in Fifth and Sixth Form will have the dance."

Elise looked confused. "Sixth Form? What *grade* is that – in plain English? I'm still not used to this system."

Ashley laughed. "I know – it takes a while, but you'll catch on. Sixth Form is like being a high school senior."

"So *they* get to have a dance. But what do we get?" Elise demanded.

"We get to watch helplessly while all the old White Oak pupils come back and invade our dorm rooms," Wendy explained.

"You're kidding!" Mary-Kate cried. "They'll be staying in our rooms?"

"No," Wendy laughed. "But they'll be prowling around the dorms and the rest of the campus all day. That's what Homecoming is all about. The pupils come back, talk over old times, and tell us how great it was when they were here."

Ashley glanced around the dorm lounge. It was a mess. The walls were only half painted. The carpeting had been ripped up. And the heavy green curtains had been pulled from the windows. They lay in a heap on the floor.

"Well, it probably *was* better in the old days!" Ashley joked. "This place is a disaster zone."

"Yeah, that's why they're redecorating," Wendy explained. "Everything has to look spiffy by the time the Homecoming crowd arrives."

Ashley stared out the window at the beautiful orange and gold leaves that covered the lawn. It was the middle of October in New Hampshire. Ivy climbed the walls of the dorms across the way.

She and Mary-Kate were completely happy at boarding school now. Sure, they missed Chicago sometimes. That's where they had grown up – and where their dad still lived.

But White Oak Academy was the best!

I love it here, Ashley thought. *But not if we have to wear uniforms!*

"I thought White Oak was totally into traditions," Ashley said. "Why would they suddenly decide to change things – and make us wear uniforms – in the middle of the school year?"

"I'm not sure," Wendy answered. "But my mom said it had something to do with a lot of girls wearing really outrageous clothes and make-up to class. And glitter," she added.

"Oops," Elise Van Hook covered her mouth and glanced at Ashley. "You mean it's all *our* fault?"

"*Your* fault," Ashley corrected her.

"Whatever," Elise said. "I wish I'd never started that stupid club, anyway."

Me, too, Ashley thought.

Elise had started a secret club a few weeks ago – right after she'd arrived at school. It was called the Glitter Girls. All the club members had to wear different coloured glitter every day.

Ashley and Mary-Kate had practically dumped

4

all their old friends to join. That was before they decided the club wasn't a good idea after all.

Luckily, everyone had forgiven them!

"I wonder what colour glitter will go with the new uniforms?" Samantha asked.

"Don't even go there!" Ashley said. "We're done with glitter. Forever."

"Well, it's not fair," Phoebe Cahill declared. "We have a right to wear what we want. It's a form of personal expression."

Phoebe was Ashley's roommate. She always wore vintage clothes – the older and more unusual, the better she liked them.

"So you're against uniforms – unless we get *vintage* ones, right?" Ashley joked.

Phoebe scrunched up her face. "Ummm, I'm not sure. What would vintage school uniforms look like?"

"Checked pleated skirts. White blouses with round collars. Knee socks and lace-up shoes," Samantha said.

"In other words, you couldn't tell them apart from brand new uniforms!" Mary-Kate joked.

"Right," Ashley agreed. She pushed a strand of her long strawberry-blonde hair out of her eyes. "That's the trouble with uniforms. They're all hopelessly out of style."

"So what are we going to do about it?" Phoebe asked.

"What *can* we do?" Samantha said.

"We can protest!" Elise suggested. "I say we all wear pyjamas to class tomorrow! That will let Mrs. Pritchard know that we won't put up with this new policy."

Mrs. Pritchard was the headmistress at White Oak. She was nice – but really strict.

Protest? Ashley thought. She and Mary-Kate exchanged glances. Did they really want to get caught up in another one of Elise's schemes?

No way, Ashley decided. Elise was fun, but her ideas were a little too far out.

But then Ashley caught the look on Phoebe's face. Her eyes had lit up at the word.

"Protest!" Phoebe cried. "What a great idea! It's so totally retro. And besides – I've got a great vintage nightgown and robe."

"I don't know," Wendy argued. "I'm not sure we'll get very far that way. I mean, if we show up for class in pyjamas, won't the Head be even more determined to make us wear uniforms?"

"And besides," Mary-Kate chimed in. "Tomorrow is Monday. We're going to Harrington – remember?"

"Good point," Ashley said.

The Harrington School for Boys was right across the road from White Oak. Ashley and Mary-Kate's cousin Jeremy was a student there. White Oak girls went over to the boys' campus two days a week, for biology lab and history classes.

"So?" Elise asked. "What's the problem?"

"I don't want to parade around in my jams in front of the guys," Mary-Kate declared.

"Especially not in front of Dylan Tunnell, right?" Ashley whispered to her sister.

"Shh!" Mary-Kate shushed her.

"Why not?" Elise asked. "I bet the guys will think it's cool."

"Have you *seen* her PJs?" Ashley cracked. "Not exactly a fashion statement. She sleeps in a Chicago Bulls T-shirt every night."

"What's wrong with that?" Mary-Kate challenged her sister.

"Nothing. It's just that it's shorter than my shortest skirt," Ashley argued. "You'll freeze!"

"True," Mary-Kate agreed.

"Okay, fine," Elise said. "You two can chicken out if you want to. But I'm doing it. I'm organising this pyjama protest – against school uniforms. Who's in?"

"Not me," Wendy said. "My mom would kill me."

"I'm up for it," Samantha volunteered. "It sounds like fun!"

"How about you, Phoebe?" Elise asked. "Are you in or out?"

Phoebe cocked her head to one side. "I'll have to think about it," she answered.

"Okay." Then Elise turned to Ashley. "Well, Ashley – what about it? Do you *really* want to just cave in to school uniforms? Just sit back and let the administration tell us what to wear – without saying a word?"

Do I? Ashley wondered.

Just giving in didn't sound like her.

Suddenly she had an idea. A brilliant idea.

"No," Ashley said. "I'm going to do something about it."

"What?" Elise asked.

Ashley smiled. "Just wait until the school newspaper comes out next week," she said. "Then you'll see!"

CHAPTER TWO

"Ashley! Whatever you do, don't stare!" Mary-Kate whispered to her sister. The two girls had just walked into biology lab on Monday morning.

"I'm not staring," Ashley answered. "I'm doing exactly what you told me – trying to see if he looks at you."

Mary-Kate stole a glance towards the crowd of boys at the front of the room. They were all huddled around something. Something near the lab table up front. Mary-Kate couldn't tell what.

Dylan Tunnell hung at the edge of the group. Mary-Kate spotted him right away. He was taller than the other guys, so his curly sandy-brown hair stood out above the crowd.

Why doesn't he ever notice me? Mary-Kate wondered. She'd noticed Dylan immediately – especially since he was the newest and cutest guy in class. She'd been trying to get his attention for two weeks.

"What's he doing?" Mary-Kate whispered to her sister.

"Smiling at something," Ashley said. "All the guys are laughing. None of them are even looking over here."

Mary-Kate turned and stared openly at the group.

"What's all the fuss?" Campbell Smith asked. Campbell was Mary-Kate's roommate.

"Who knows? Maybe there's a frog up there or something" Ashley guessed.

Just then the crowd of guys parted. Now Mary-Kate could *see* what the fuss was about.

It wasn't a frog – that was for sure.

Elise, Samantha and a girl named Brittany were all standing there – in their PJs!

"I can't believe it," Ashley whispered. "Elise actually wore her satin nightgown to class!"

"At least she has her coat on over it," Phoebe said.

"I'm surprised the bus driver let her on the shuttle," Campbell chimed in.

"Who – Gordon? He keeps his eyes on the road," Ashley said. "He probably didn't even notice."

Mary-Kate tried to concentrate on Dylan. She only had two chances each week to get his attention. She didn't want to waste this one.

Mary-Kate pulled out a pencil and headed for the pencil sharpener. She had to pass by Dylan to get there.

Okay, so it's the oldest trick in the book, she thought. *Marching past a guy's desk. Who cares, if it works!*

"Excuse me," she said. She scooted past him and edged around the lab table.

Dylan moved, but didn't even make eye contact.

Mary-Kate's heart sank. *Doesn't he even know I'm alive?*

She sharpened her pencil and started back to her seat. This time, she didn't say "excuse me". She tried to bump into him – but just a little. Just enough to brush his arm.

"Oh, sorry," she said.

"No problem," Dylan muttered, not looking up.

What do I have to do to get his attention – knock him down? she wondered.

She kept her eyes glued on Dylan as she walked towards her seat. She hoped he'd turn around and notice her.

That's why she didn't see where she was going—and didn't see Marty Silver in her path. He was the only guy in the whole school who was shorter than Mary-Kate.

"Hey, watch out!" Marty cried as he tripped, trying to get out of her way.

He crashed to the floor, loudly knocking over two lab stools.

Everyone turned to stare. All the guys, including Dylan, burst out laughing.

"Way to make an entrance, Marty!" someone called out.

"She knocked me down!" Marty whined as he pulled himself to his feet.

The crowd of guys at the front broke up and wandered to their seats. Dylan sauntered over towards Mary-Kate.

"Oh, right," he said to Marty with a laugh. "Big strong Ashley Burke knocked you down with a feather."

He flashed Mary-Kate a smile.

"I'm not Ashley," she said. "I'm Mary-Kate."

"Oh, yeah?" Dylan frowned and stared at her as if he was trying to figure something out. He seemed to be checking out her clothes. "Huh. Don't you write a fashion column for the White Oak newspaper?"

"No. That's my sister," Mary-Kate said. "But sometimes I write a sports column," she added.

Dylan shrugged. "Oh, well," he mumbled. "I'll never be able to tell you two apart." He paused. "Unless . . ."

Mary-Kate's eyes lit up. "Unless what?" *I'll do anything to get him to notice me!* she thought.

"Unless you get a tattoo!" he joked, laughing hard at the idea.

Mary-Kate laughed, too. But inside she was totally bummed out. *He's right*, she decided. *He can't tell us apart, because I look so much like Ashley.*

But I could change that – if I changed the way I dress. I need my own look!

Just then Mr. Barber, the bio teacher, walked in. "Well," he said, staring at Elise, Samantha and Brittany. "I know you girls usually sleep through my class. Now I see you've come dressed for it!"

Everyone laughed and sat down.

"But seriously," Mr. Barber went on. "Pyjamas are not the proper attire for class. I understand that it's some sort of protest, so I'll allow it today. But this had better be the first and last time."

Mary-Kate plopped on to the stool between her lab partner, Rebecca, and Rebecca's best friend,

Poppy. The two of them always drove Mary-Kate crazy – because they talked *around* her.

"I love Elise's nightgown!" Rebecca whispered, leaning behind Mary-Kate. "I want one just like it."

"If I win that contest at the mall on Saturday, I'm going to buy one," Poppy whispered back. "Maybe they have it in blue."

"If I win, I'm getting a whole new wardrobe," Rebecca said.

"We'll never win," Poppy said. "Unless we get there early."

"What contest?" Mary-Kate blurted out.

Whoops! I wasn't supposed to be part of that conversation! she realised. *Oh, well.*

Rebecca glared at Mary-Kate, then shot a glance at Poppy. "Should we tell her?"

Poppy shrugged. "I don't care. We aren't really going to win anyway. There will probably be hundreds of people there. One more won't hurt."

"Okay," Rebecca gave in. "There's a shopping-spree contest at the mall. It starts at noon. If you win, you get a complete makeover – and a gift certificate for three hundred dollars worth of clothes from any of the stores in the mall."

"Wow," Mary-Kate said. "Cool. What do you have to do to win?"

"I'm not sure. It's a scavenger hunt of some kind," Rebecca explained.

A scavenger hunt? I'm pretty good at finding things, Mary-Kate thought. *I bet I can win.*

"Okay, class, take out your diagrams of the human body," Mr. Barber said.

Class was about to start. But Mary-Kate couldn't concentrate. She kept staring at the back of Dylan's head. He was *so* cute.

She drew curly hair on her diagram of the respiratory system. Then she took out a sheet of paper and wrote a note to her sister.

"Guess what?" the note said. "There's a shopping-spree contest at the mall on Saturday. I'm going to enter it – and win! Then I'll get a whole new look, and Dylan will finally notice me."

Ashley scribbled on the note and passed it back to Mary-Kate. "Wake up," it said. "You're dreaming. In two weeks we'll all be wearing school uniforms every day. What good will a shopping spree do then?"

Oh, no! Mary-Kate realised as she crumpled up the note. *Ashley's right!*

Once they started wearing uniforms, she and Ashley would be dressed exactly alike.

Every single day of their lives.

And then Dylan would *never* be able to tell them apart!

CHAPTER THREE

As soon as bio was over, Ashley raced out of the classroom. She hurried to find Phoebe, so they could sit together on the bus back to White Oak.

Phoebe was wearing a funny flannel shirt – brown, with little old-fashioned aeroplanes on it. She had it tucked into her jeans. Vintage white Levi's from the 1960s.

"We've got to talk," Ashley said. "About this dress code problem."

"It's more than a dress code," Phoebe exclaimed. "It's school uniforms! I had a terrible nightmare about it last night."

"Really?" Ashley wasn't surprised. The whole thing seemed like a nightmare to her too.

"I dreamed I saw the new uniforms," Phoebe explained. "They were black and white striped trousers and tops. Like *prison* uniforms!"

Ashley nodded with a shudder. "I know. Not being able to wear fashionable clothes is like a life sentence to me."

"So what are we going to do?" Phoebe asked. "You said you had an idea."

"I do," Ashley leaned in close. "I thought about it all night. We've got to write an article about it in the school newspaper – in our fashion column. We'll take a stand against the new uniforms. Maybe we can get the whole school behind us."

"Then the board of trustees will *have* to change their minds!" Phoebe exclaimed.

"Exactly," Ashley said with a big smile.

Phoebe gave Ashley a high-five and grinned, too. "Count me in," she said. "We should talk to Mrs. Bloomberg about it as soon as we get back."

Great, Ashley thought. She felt really good about her plan. She and Phoebe climbed on the shuttle bus and headed for the back.

She couldn't wait to write her article. As soon as the news about the school uniforms got out, the whole school would be in an uproar.

And she, Ashley Burke, would be the brilliant reporter who broke the story and saved the day!

17

As soon as they pulled into the White Oak campus, Ashley and Phoebe hurried to find Mrs. Bloomberg. Mrs. Bloomberg was their English teacher. She was also the adviser for the school newspaper. She had to approve each article before it went into print.

At least I'm finally on her good side, Ashley thought as they entered the teacher's office. Mrs. Bloomberg was really strict. Ashley had worked hard to win her approval.

"Hello, girls," Mrs. Bloomberg said. "I was just leaving. What can I help you with that won't take more than five minutes?"

Quickly the girls explained their idea for a column about the school uniforms.

Mrs. Bloomberg scowled. "I hadn't even heard about this," she said. "Uniforms? Here at White Oak?"

"I know!" Phoebe chimed in. "Isn't it terrible?"

"I don't know if it's terrible," Mrs. Bloomberg replied. "But it certainly is quite a surprise. Well, you girls have my permission to go ahead with a column. Now, which one of you is going to take the 'pro' position, and which one will take the 'con'?"

"Pro?" Ashley said with a gulp. "Neither of us! We're both totally opposed."

Mrs. Bloomberg frowned again. "I understand that, Ashley. But we can't have an article that's

18

one-sided. Both points of view must be represented. One of you will have to make the argument in favour of uniforms."

"Not me," Ashley declared. "I'm totally against them. And besides, this article was my idea."

"But I'm the one who had nightmares last night!" Phoebe argued. "I hate the idea of uniforms more than anyone. And besides – you didn't even join in the protest today. I did."

Ashley's eyes opened wide. *"You* wore pyjamas to class?" she asked. "What pyjamas?"

Phoebe got a hurt look on her face. "This!" she cried, pointing at her brown flannel shirt. "It's a boy's pyjama top from the 1950s."

Ashley rolled her eyes. "Well that doesn't count!" she argued. "No one could tell it was pyjamas."

Mrs. Bloomberg looked irritated. "Girls, girls," she said firmly. "I can't listen to this any longer. I've got to go. Ashley – you take the 'pro' position. Phoebe, you take the 'con'. It's settled."

Then she picked up her things and marched out.

Not fair, Ashley thought as she sat at her computer that night. *Here I am, stuck writing an article in favour of school uniforms. And I hate the idea!*

Still, she couldn't help putting her best efforts

into the article. After all, writing was one of her main talents. She always did a good job on book reports and columns for the newspaper.

And my headline is so cool! Ashley thought. "*FIRST FORM FOR UNIFORMS.*"

I'll bet Phoebe doesn't come up with anything as good as this.

Ashley made a list of all the arguments in favour of school uniforms, then read it over.

"My list of pros is too convincing," Ashley muttered out loud.

Phoebe glanced up from her desk, across the room.

"Don't worry," Phoebe said. "I've got the cons covered."

"I know you'll do a good job," Ashley said. "That's not what I'm worried about. What if people think I'm actually in favour of uniforms?"

"Yeah, that would be bad," Phoebe agreed. "Totally embarrassing."

Yikes, Ashley thought. *This whole thing could really backfire. Everyone in the whole school could think she was on the wrong side!*

Her stomach did a flip-flop. *Oh, well,* she decided. She'd just tell everyone how Mrs. Bloomberg made her take that side of the issue.

They'll have to understand. Won't they?

20

CHAPTER FOUR

"Oh my gosh – no!"

Dana Woletsky's shriek carried halfway across the dining hall.

Ashley held a bite of oatmeal midway to her mouth. She lowered her spoon, turned and stared.

"What's wrong with *her*?" Ashley asked.

Mary-Kate sipped her OJ. "Who knows," she said. "Maybe someone just told her how many calories there are in one of these blueberry muffins."

Ashley laughed at her sister's joke. They both felt the same way about Dana. She was pretty and popular – but totally stuck up. And sneaky. No one trusted her.

"At least we *get* blueberry muffins on Saturday," Ashley said. "Instead of just plain old traditional White Oak oatmeal. But what's she so upset about?"

Campbell craned her neck to see Dana. "She's reading something," Campbell reported. "I think it's the White Oak *Acorn*. Is it out already?"

"Oh, wow!" Ashley jumped up. "I'll go and see!"

Ashley darted across the dining hall to the lobby. A stack of newly printed newspapers had just been deposited on a table near the door. She grabbed three copies and hurried back inside.

"Check this out," Ashley said when she reached her table. "Our school uniforms article is on the second page!"

Mary-Kate and Campbell both snatched copies of the newspaper from Ashley's hands. All three were silent as they read.

"You know, you're right, Ashley," Campbell announced when she'd finished reading. "Uniforms are a *great* idea! They'll make my life so much simpler."

"Don't say that!" Ashley cried. "I told you – I don't believe a word I wrote!"

"I know, but I still agree with you! If we get uniforms, I won't even have to *think* about what to wear each day!" Campbell declared.

Ashley rolled her eyes and stuffed another spoonful of oatmeal in her mouth. *Great!* she thought. *Now I've got Campbell on my side!*

Campbell was nice enough, in Ashley's opinion. But she was even more of a jock than Mary-Kate. Definitely not into fashion. So her opinion about clothes didn't really count.

Ashley was about to take another bite when someone smacked her on the head – with a newspaper.

"Ow!" Ashley said, whirling around.

Wendy and Sarabeth Ang stood right behind her, scowling.

"I read your column," Wendy said. "Wow. I never thought you'd change your mind like that!"

"I didn't!" Ashley cried. "Mrs. Bloomberg made me write it that way. I'm totally against uniforms!"

"You are?" Wendy's eyes opened wider. "Well, it sure doesn't sound that way."

Ashley's face fell. "I know. But you believe me, don't you?"

Wendy nodded. "I guess."

Two girls from Second Form got up from their table. With their trays in their hands, they turned to Ashley.

"Did you write this article in favour of school uniforms?" one of them asked.

Ashley sighed. "No. I mean, yes, but I'm really against them."

The girl shot Ashley a puzzled look. "Weird. Then why did you say you were for them in the paper?"

"I didn't!" Ashley tried to explain. "All I did was point out why some people think they're a good idea. Mrs. Bloomberg made me . . ."

But the girls were already walking away.

"This is the pits," Ashley moaned. "Everyone thinks I'm in favour of uniforms!"

"It's just because you're such a good writer," Mary-Kate said. "You were really convincing."

Ashley shot her sister a grateful smile. "Thanks for trying to cheer me up," she said. "But—"

"Uh-oh," Campbell interrupted. "Here comes Dana and her posse."

Ashley braced herself. Dana could be so awful, when she wanted to be. And she was headed straight for Ashley's table.

"They're coming this way on purpose," Mary-Kate whispered. "It's not even on the way to the door."

"Ignore them," Ashley whispered back.

But that was hard to do. Dana was talking loudly to her friends. She was practically broadcasting her opinions to everyone in the dining hall.

"No, no," Dana announced loudly. "I mean, you've got to understand Ashley's point of view. She'll certainly look *better* in a school uniform than she does in her *own* clothes!"

All the girls with Dana laughed. A few older girls overheard it. They glanced at Ashley, too.

Ashley was mortified.

"Get me out of here!" she whispered to Mary-Kate.

But just then two more girls approached their table. "Is it true?" Lexy Martin asked. "Are we getting school uniforms?"

"Gosh, I hope not!" Ashley said. "Wouldn't that be the worst?"

"Not according to your article," Lexy shot back. She gave Ashley a strange look.

"I didn't really mean what I wrote," Ashley tried to explain for the fourth time. "It's just that Mrs. Bloomberg made me take that side . . ."

Her voice trailed off. *Why go on?* she thought. They weren't even listening. Lexy and the other girl had already walked away.

Ashley stood up and lifted her tray. She wasn't hungry any more.

"I'm getting out of here," she announced.

"Wait!" Mary-Kate called. "Aren't you coming with me to the mall? The shuttle bus leaves in fifteen minutes."

The mall? Ashley had almost forgotten. Today was the day of the big shopping-spree contest! That would definitely be more fun than hanging around school and trying to explain that article to everyone.

"Okay," she replied. "I'll come."

"Good," Mary-Kate said. "Then you'll be there to congratulate me when I win!"

"We'll see about that," Ashley said.

"What do you mean?" Mary-Kate looked puzzled.

"It's just that if you're going to win," Ashley explained, "you'll have to beat *me* first!"

CHAPTER FIVE

"Hold on," Mary-Kate stopped dead in her tracks. "*You're* entering the contest at the mall, too?"

"Of course," Ashley replied. "A shopping spree? It sounds fabulous!"

"But *I'm* the one who needs the makeover!" Mary-Kate protested. "And you wouldn't even know about the contest if it weren't for me!"

"So what?" Ashley said. "*You* wouldn't know about it if Rebecca and Poppy hadn't told you – right?"

Mary-Kate was silent. She couldn't argue with that.

"Come on," Ashley said. "If we don't hurry, we'll miss the bus!"

Mary-Kate grabbed her jacket and followed her sister towards the door. They climbed on the bus together and rode to the mall.

Mary-Kate stared out the window on the way. The autumn leaves floated down from the trees and decorated the winding roads.

Okay, she thought. *Ashley's in a bad mood about her article in the school paper. I can sympathise with that. But that's no reason to spoil my plans and my whole day!*

"It's not fair," Mary-Kate said as they pulled into the mall parking lot. "I mean, you know why I need to win this contest. So I'll get a new wardrobe and Dylan will notice me."

"Don't worry," Ashley answered, getting off the bus. She hurried towards the mall entrance. "He'll notice you next week, whether you win or not."

"How come?" Mary-Kate asked.

"Because if I win, I'll have all new clothes!" Ashley joked. "And you'll be wearing the same old things. Then he'll definitely be able to tell us apart!"

"That's not funny," Mary-Kate called. She ran to catch up with her sister. "Ashley – wait! We have to talk!"

Mary-Kate gasped as she followed her sister into the mall. It was packed with people. There was a big table in the centre. The sign over it said: WIN A SHOPPING SPREE! SIGN UP HERE.

"Whoa!" Ashley said, staring at the crowds. "There must be three hundred people here!"

"At least," Mary-Kate agreed. Her hopes sank. "How am I going to beat all these people at the scavenger hunt?"

"I've got an idea," Ashley answered, pulling her sister aside.

"What?" Mary-Kate waited. She was willing to do anything – anything! But she had to win.

"We can double our chances of winning, if we work together," Ashley suggested. "And if we win, we'll split the prize."

"Split it? I don't know," Mary-Kate said. "I mean, how am I going to get a whole new look that way?"

"You'll get *half* a new look," Ashley said.

Half a look? Would that be enough to catch Dylan's eye? Mary-Kate wasn't sure. But with so many people competing for the prize, she had little chance of winning, anyway.

Maybe it *was* better to share the job – and the prize – with Ashley.

"Look, let's just win," Ashley argued. "Then we can decide how to split up the prize later."

"Okay – I guess," Mary-Kate agreed. "You get in line. I'll go get a copy of the rules."

Ashley nodded and took a place in line. Twenty people were ahead of them, including Rebecca and Poppy from school. They were all waiting to sign up for the contest.

Mary-Kate raced to the front of the table and grabbed two of the sign-up sheets. Her heart was fluttering with excitement.

Wow, she thought as she read the rules. The contest was really going to be fun!

It was a find-the-bears contest. There were five stuffed animals hidden in five different stores throughout the mall. Each bear was a different colour and had a different number on it.

"See?" Mary-Kate said, explaining the contest to Ashley. "The bears are numbered from one to five. And each one is a different colour – red, yellow, green, blue and brown. You have to write down the name of the store where you find each bear on this sheet – along with its colour and number. That way, people can't just guess."

"Cool," Ashley said. "But does it say where the bears are? I mean, are they in the window or what?"

Mary-Kate scoffed. "No way! That's the whole point of the contest. We have to go into all these stores and look around. It's a gimmick – to get people into stores they'd never dream of shopping in."

"Smart," Ashley agreed.

"Anyway, I've figured it out," Mary-Kate said. "We'll split up. I'll take the upper level of the mall. You take the lower level. We'll meet back at the escalator every fifteen minutes. When we have all five bears – we'll win."

Mary-Kate glanced at the clock. The contest would start in ten minutes – exactly at noon.

Both girls quickly filled out the sign-up sheets. Then they got into position, near the escalator.

"Ladies, gentlemen and young people," a man said over the loudspeaker system in the mall. "The find-the-bears contest will begin in one minute. You'll hear a bell. That signals the bears are waiting for you. Good luck to everyone!"

When the bell sounded, Mary-Kate took off. She ran up the escalator to the top level of the mall.

Where should I look first? she wondered.

The closest store was a gift shop. They had lots of little carved wooden animals and porcelain vases from Asia in the window.

Mary-Kate dashed inside and glanced around. "Any bears in here?" she asked the clerk.

"I'm not allowed to say," the clerk answered. "But we're having a sale on those carved boxes . . ."

"Maybe later," Mary-Kate said quickly. She scanned the store quickly. Nope – no bears.

Her heart pounded as she dashed out of the store and into a running-shoe shop next door. The place was packed with customers. Huge guys from a nearby high school were standing around, gawking at the latest hiking boots.

Mary-Kate had to squeeze between them to get through. She raced to the back of the store, looking everywhere.

High and low.

Nothing. She was about to leave, when she spotted something blue sitting at the very top of the wall of shoes.

The blue bear was up there. He had a number 5 on his chest.

"Aha!" she almost blurted out.

Quickly, she clamped a hand over her mouth. What if other scavenger hunters overheard her? She didn't want to give any clues away!

Mary-Kate found an empty corner of the store and knelt down on the rug. She scribbled the store's name on the form, next to number 5. Then she wrote in the colour – blue.

One down, four to go! she thought as she dashed out of the store. But the next six stores she went into were losers. No bears. And it was time to meet Ashley.

She ran to the escalator. Ashley was waiting at the top.

"I've got one," Mary-Kate announced.

"I've got two!" Ashley cried.

"Great!" Mary-Kate said. "See you in fifteen!"

Ashley hurried back down the escalator, and Mary-Kate dashed off. This time she started on the other side of the hall. She raced into a bookstore and headed to the back – to the children's section.

Isn't that where they'd put a bear? she thought.

Besides – something yellow was sticking out into the aisle.

Mary-Kate's heart thumped. She ran to get the bear's number. *I'm going to win!* she thought.

But it was only a Winnie the Pooh bear – sitting next to a display of Winnie the Pooh books. It didn't have a number on it.

"Oh, man," Mary-Kate moaned. She was starting to feel discouraged.

Mary-Kate raced out of the store and darted in and out of the next three shops wildly. Finally she spotted something. Something brown, sitting under a man's hat in a fancy men's clothing store.

Wow, Mary-Kate thought. *That's cheating!* You could hardly see the bear.

She slipped behind the counter and stood on tiptoes to peek under the hat.

Yes! It was a bear, with a number 3 on his chest!

Mary-Kate's eyes darted around the store, to be sure no one was watching her. She wrote the colour brown on her entry form, next to number 3. Then she wrote "Mark Miles". That was the name of the store.

I've got two, she thought, running out.

She raced out of the store and stared down the mall. *Where to next?* she wondered.

Just then she spotted two women coming out of a candy store. They looked excited. And they were holding entry forms in their hands!

I'll bet there's a bear in there, Mary-Kate thought. She ran into the candy store.

Sure enough, a red bear was stuffed inside the clear plastic bin full of red licorice. The licorice was wrapped around his head and legs. But Mary-Kate could still see him. He had a number 2 on his chest.

Mary-Kate couldn't wait to get back to the escalator. Ashley was already at the top, waiting for her.

"I've got three!" Mary-Kate cried. "We win! Give me your other two, so I can copy them on my entry form!"

"Wait – *I've* got three," Ashley argued.

Huh? How could Ashley find three of the bears on the lower level? There were only two down there. The other three were upstairs.

"I have the yellow bear, the green one and the blue one," Ashley began.

"We'll argue about it later," Mary-Kate cried. "Just give me your form, before someone else beats us to it!"

Ashley handed the form to her sister. Then they both ran to the sign-up table as fast as they could. Frantically Mary-Kate scribbled the rest of the answers on her own form. She shoved it to the man in charge.

He glanced at it quickly and smiled.

"Well, young lady, it looks like we've got a winner!" he said.

"Yes!" Mary-Kate shouted. "I knew I'd win!"

"Ladies, gentlemen and young people," the man said through the loudspeaker. "The find-the-bears contest is over. Mary-Kate Burke has won – in record time, I might add. But thank you all for playing. And have a good shopping day."

He shook Mary-Kate's hand.

"Ashley – we have to talk," Mary-Kate said, pulling her sister aside. "How did you find the blue bear? It was upstairs. You must have been hunting on the upper level."

"I was," Ashley admitted. "But that's only because I heard a man say the blue bear was in Shoes for Sure. I already had the yellow and green – so I figured I'd go where the action was. To help us both win."

"That makes sense," Mary-Kate said. "I would have done the same thing. But still – I'm the one who found the blue bear first. And I *really* need this shopping spree. I think I should get more of the prize money."

Ashley eyed her sister. "You really want a new wardrobe, don't you?"

Mary-Kate nodded. "And the makeover. I've got to do it – for Dylan's sake."

Ashley put her arm around her sister and smiled. "Come on. The judges are waiting to give you your prize. You can have the whole thing."

"Really? Thanks!" Mary-Kate beamed. "You're the best!"

"I just hope Dylan notices you on Monday – after all this," Ashley said.

"Oh, he'll notice me," Mary-Kate promised. "Just wait. I'm going to make *sure* of that!"

CHAPTER
SIX

"Ashley! Mary-Kate! Where have you been? I've been looking all over for you!" Wendy called, running up to them.

The girls had just stepped off the shuttle bus coming back from the mall. It was late Saturday afternoon. A chilly October wind blew.

"We went to the mall, and Mary-Kate won the shopping spree!" Ashley announced. "And a makeover! Look at her – doesn't she look fabulous?"

Wendy glanced at Mary-Kate, checking her out up and down. "Faded jeans and a Chicago Bulls T-shirt?" Wendy said. "That's a *makeover?*"

"Not the clothes!" Mary-Kate sighed. "We ran

out of time, so I had to save the shopping spree till next weekend. But they did my make-up – and gave me a whole bag of make-up products to keep." She held it up for everyone to see. "What do you think?"

Wendy nodded. "The make-up is good," she said. "Perfect. You can hardly tell you're wearing any – which is the way models do it."

Mary-Kate frowned. "If you can't tell, how is Dylan going to notice?" she mumbled.

"You'll have to work on it," Ashley advised. "Maybe use a little bit more. But not too much. It's tricky."

"Well, at least you're back," Wendy went on. "I have news. Big news. The school uniforms are here!"

Ashley gulped. "They are? Where?"

"In Mrs. Pritchard's office," Wendy replied. "I just talked to my mom. She said a sample uniform was dropped off for the Head today."

"Oh, my gosh," Ashley said. "I'm dying to see it."

"So am I," Wendy agreed. "That's why I've been looking for you. Let's go over there right now and see how it looks!"

"What – just walk into the Head's office and demand to see it?" Ashley asked.

"Why not?" Wendy said. "I mean, of course we'd

ask nicely. But we have a right to know what the uniforms are going to look like. Don't we?"

"I guess so," Ashley decided. She pulled her jacket around her tightly to keep out the cold air. "Okay, let's go."

All three girls marched toward the main building.

Joan, Mrs. Pritchard's secretary, smiled at them as they walked in. Ashley was surprised to see her. Joan didn't usually work on Saturdays.

"Hello, girls," Joan said. "Mrs. Pritchard isn't here. Did you have an appointment with her?"

"No," Ashley said. "But we, uh . . ."

"We were hoping to talk to her," Wendy chimed in.

Joan checked the Head's schedule. "She won't be back for a while. She went out to do some errands. But you're welcome to wait."

Ashley glanced towards Mrs. Pritchard's office door. She couldn't really see inside.

Was the new uniform in there?

"We'll wait," Ashley offered.

"Fine," Joan said. "Just have a seat."

Ashley and Mary-Kate sat down on the hard bench near the wall. They sat quietly, watching the clock. Twenty minutes went by. It drove Ashley

39

crazy, listening to Joan clicking away on her computer keyboard.

"Do you think she'll be back soon?" Ashley asked.

Joan shook her head. "Hard to know," she answered. "I'm sorry I can't be more help."

Ashley checked the clock again. Three thirty. They'd been waiting forty minutes.

Was the Head ever coming back?

"Excuse me, girls," Joan said, standing up. "I've got to take these files over to the librarian's office. I'll be right back."

Ashley nodded politely. She kept her face calm until Joan had put on her coat and left. Then she jumped up.

"Let's sneak in there!" she whispered. "And get a look at that new uniform while we have the chance!"

"Do we dare?" Mary-Kate asked.

"Yes!" Ashley and Wendy both said at once.

They dashed into Mrs. Pritchard's office. Mary-Kate was right behind them.

The afternoon sun was low in the sky, so Mrs. Pritchard's office was dark. Ashley quickly flipped on a light. There, hanging on the back of a closet door, was the new school uniform.

"Oh my gosh – it's hideous!" Ashley cried.

Her mouth hung open. It was even worse than she had imagined!

The uniform was a horrible bright green jumper with a box-pleated skirt. The white blouse had little green oak leaves embroidered on the collar.

And there was a note attached to it. A handwritten note.

Mary-Kate read it aloud.

Dear Mrs. Pritchard,

I'm so very pleased to have had the chance to design the new school uniforms for my beloved White Oak Academy. I'm sure the girls will be thrilled with the new look – it features the school colours. Please let me know if there is anything else I can do for our dear alma mater. I look forward to seeing you at Homecoming.

Best wishes always,
Mrs. Claudia Wainwright

Ashley was stunned. She didn't know what to say. Could Mrs. Pritchard really expect them to wear that thing? She'd die if she had to wear it even once. Let alone every day!

"What are we going to do?" Mary-Kate cried. "It's so . . . so . . ."

"Ugly," Ashley finished her sister's sentence. "I think that's the word you're looking for."

"Right," Mary-Kate agreed. "I mean, even a supermodel would look like a munchkin from the *Wizard of Oz* in that thing!"

"The munchkins wore blue," Ashley corrected her sister.

"Well, those guys in the Emerald City didn't," Mary-Kate argued.

"Anyway, it's hideous," Wendy said. "No matter who wears it."

Phoebe was right, Ashley thought. *This is a nightmare. If only they'd wake up!*

Ashley ran to the window to look outside. Joan was already heading back.

"Uh-oh. We'd better get out of here," Ashley said. "Before she comes back."

"Before *who* comes back?" a voice behind them asked.

Ashley whirled around. Her heart skipped a beat.

Standing there in the doorway was Mrs. Pritchard herself. They'd been caught snooping around in the headmistress's office – by the Head!

CHAPTER SEVEN

"What, may I ask, are you girls doing in here?" Mrs. Pritchard demanded.

Ashley's face flushed red. "Uh, well, to tell you the truth, Mrs. Pritchard, it's a long story."

Mrs. Pritchard frowned. "I'm listening," she said. "Go on."

Ashley's brain whirred. What should she say? Finally she decided to just tell the truth – more or less.

"Well, Wendy heard that the new school uniform had arrived," Ashley explained. "So we came to ask you if we could see it. But then we got tired of waiting and decided to leave you a note. To ask if we could come see the uniform another time. But

Joan was gone, and we didn't have any paper, so we came into your office to look for some . . . and that's when you came back."

Mrs. Pritchard cocked her head to one side. "I see," she said. She eyed Ashley for a long moment. "Well, next time, I'd prefer you to wait for Joan to come back. I don't appreciate having girls letting themselves into my office when I'm not here, all right?"

"Of course," Ashley said quickly.

Mary-Kate and Wendy nodded in agreement, too.

"But as long as you're here now," Mrs. Pritchard went on, "why don't you look at the uniform? I'd love to know what you girls think."

Ashley turned towards the closet door and swallowed hard.

"Honestly?" Ashley asked.

"Yes," the Head said with a nod.

"I don't like it," Ashley declared. "And I don't think anyone else will like it either."

Mrs. Pritchard seemed truly surprised. "You don't? Why not?"

"It's out of date," Ashley explained. "Totally out of style. And the colours are terrible. No one looks good in bright green."

Mary-Kate gave Ashley a nudge. Whoops! Ashley suddenly noticed that Mrs. Pritchard's blouse was almost the same colour green!

"I mean, *most* people don't," Ashley added quickly.

"I see," Mrs. Pritchard said again. She frowned and paced the room. "Well, I must say I'm surprised. I thought Mrs. Wainwright had a good sense of style. I remember she was always one of the best-dressed women at Homecoming in past years."

"Maybe so," Mary-Kate said, chiming in. "But she's not our age."

"That's true," Mrs. Pritchard said with a small smile.

"Um, Mrs. Pritchard, may I make a suggestion?" Ashley asked.

"All right," the Head answered. "What is it?"

"Would you be willing to consider another design for the uniform?"

"What kind of design?" Mrs. Pritchard asked.

"I'm not sure yet," Ashley admitted. "But I think if I had a few days, I could come up with something that everyone at school would like."

Why not? Ashley thought. *With my fashion sense, I should be able to design something that's both classic and stylish. Shouldn't I?*

Mrs. Pritchard thought for a minute. "Well," she said finally, "all right. I'll give you until Wednesday. If you can come up with a reasonable alternative, I'll let you present it to the whole school at the assembly. And then we'll see."

"Thank you!" Ashley said, jumping up a little. She almost reached over and hugged the Head.

"Now, if you'll excuse me, girls," Mrs. Pritchard said, "I have some work to do."

Ashley and Mary-Kate grinned at each other as they hurried out the door.

"Yes!" Wendy said, giving Ashley high fives. "You've done it! You've saved us from munchkinville!"

"Not quite," Ashley said. "I still have to come up with a new uniform. And we're *still* going to have to wear uniforms every day – remember?"

"That's okay," Wendy shot back. "As long as it's not that green and white thing, I can stand it."

Not too *much pressure!* Ashley thought.

But Ashley was excited. If she could come up with a great uniform, she'd be the most popular girl in the whole school!

CHAPTER EIGHT

"Too fashionable," Mary-Kate commented when Ashley popped into her room later that night.

Ashley stood in the doorway modelling an outfit – the fifth one she'd come up with so far. She was trying out ideas for the new school uniform. Mary-Kate was acting as judge, jury and executioner.

"What's wrong with black slim-legged trousers and a cropped pink cashmere sweater?" Ashley argued.

"Well, for one thing, I'd say the three-inch platform shoes are a long shot," Campbell answered from her bunk bed.

"And the cashmere isn't practical," Mary-Kate explained. "The Head will never approve it."

"But it's so . . . so quietly chic!" Ashley cooed.

"Give it up, Ashley," Mary-Kate counselled her. "It's too casual, too expensive, and . . ."

"Too pink!" Campbell chimed in.

"Okay. I'll try again," Ashley said, sulking. "But I really liked this one."

"Don't worry. You've still got two more days to come up with the perfect outfit," Mary-Kate said.

She watched her sister trudge back to her own dorm room.

"Ashley's beginning to panic," Mary-Kate confided to Campbell when her sister was gone.

"How come?" Campbell asked. "I mean, Ashley loves clothes. This should be the perfect job for her."

"I think it's turning out to be harder than she thought," Mary-Kate guessed. "Most of her clothes are too something. Too colourful to look good on everyone. Or too fashionable to be in style for more than the next five minutes. Or too extreme to wear every day."

"Maybe you'd better help her," Campbell said.

Me? Mary-Kate thought. *I can't give anyone fashion advice. I'm still trying to find a look of my own!*

Still, she wanted to be there for her sister.

And besides – she wanted to get Ashley's advice, too. About her make-up. So she'd be all ready to impress Dylan tomorrow.

48

Mary-Kate hurried to the mirror with all her new make-up products.

Carefully she applied blush to her cheeks. Then she stroked on some light brown eyebrow pencil. A thin line of brown eyeliner was the finishing touch.

"Be back soon," Mary-Kate told Campbell.

She padded down the hall to her sister's room and popped into Ashley's doorway.

"What do you think of this?" Mary-Kate asked.

Ashley whirled around. She eyed her sister up and down. "Sweat pants and a stained sweatshirt? As a school uniform?" she gasped. "I'd rather wear the green munchkin thing!"

"Not my *clothes*!" Mary-Kate rolled her eyes. "My make-up! I'm trying out the things I got at the mall."

"Oh – it looks great," Ashley said.

"Really?"

But Ashley wasn't listening. She was staring into her closet with a desperate look on her face. Then she glanced at her bed. Half her wardrobe was spread out there.

"Try something more conservative," Mary-Kate suggested. "How about the grey checked skirt?"

Ashley wrinkled up her nose. "Ew, no," she said.

"I don't have a thing that goes with it. And besides – it's too . . . boring."

Phoebe lifted her eyes from her book. She was sprawled on her own bed, across the room. "How about that funky skirt with the beaded fringe? Put that with a plain black top and see how it looks."

Ashley looked questioningly at her sister.

"The Head would never go for beaded," Mary-Kate advised. "It's got to be something classic."

Phoebe shrugged and went back to reading poetry. "Well, classic is your department, Ashley – not mine. Good luck."

"That's what I'm going to need!" Ashley moaned. "Luck!"

Mary-Kate stared into her own closet the next morning.

Now I know how Ashley felt last night, she thought. *I have nothing to wear! Nothing that will really grab Dylan's attention.*

It was Monday morning, and Mary-Kate had already missed breakfast to work on her make-up. She wanted to look fabulous when they arrived at Harrington for bio lab. She had spent forty minutes on her face so far. It still didn't look right.

Her stomach growled.

"Mary-Kate! The shuttle bus leaves in five minutes!" Campbell called, dashing back into their room.

"I know, I know, I'm hurrying!" Mary-Kate said. "But I can't make decisions on an empty stomach. I'm starving."

"I sneaked you a piece of fruit and dry toast from the dining hall." Campbell handed over a napkin wrapped around some food.

Mary-Kate chomped on the banana, crunched on the toast and grabbed a pair of lavender corduroys from her closet. She tossed on a matching lavender pullover sweater.

"Does this look okay?" she asked.

"You're asking *me*?" Campbell replied. "Isn't that kind of like asking Ashley for advice on throwing a fastball?"

"I guess so," Mary-Kate agreed with a laugh.

She grabbed her coat and they ran for the shuttle bus.

I hope this works! Mary-Kate thought all the way over to the Harrington School.

When she walked into biology lab, Dylan was already in his seat. He was working away on the homework for the day – a diagram of the heart.

He didn't look up until class started.

Mary-Kate could hardly concentrate on bio. She was too busy trying to send Dylan an ESP message.

Turn around, she thought, concentrating on the back of his head. *Turn around and notice me!*

Finally class was over. Mary-Kate leaped out of her seat and rushed to be near him.

"Hi!" she said, trying to act casual.

"Oh, hi, Ashley," he replied. "I read your article in the White Oak *Acorn*. It was really good."

"I'm Mary-Kate!" she blurted out.

But Dylan didn't hear her. The hallway was noisy, and Dylan had already turned away.

Mary-Kate ran to catch up with Ashley. "I'm going to die," she announced.

"What's wrong?" Ashley asked.

"Dylan didn't even notice my new make-up!" Mary-Kate moaned.

Ashley squinted. "What make-up?"

"You can't see it?" Mary-Kate asked. "I worked on it for almost an hour!"

"Too natural," Ashley announced. "You need more."

Okay, that's it! Mary-Kate decided. *I'm going all out from now on. I'll make sure Dylan notices me next time – no matter what I have to do!*

CHAPTER NINE

"Ashley! Your clock went off twenty minutes ago!" Phoebe gently prodded her roommate.

Ashley rolled over in bed and moaned.

Her head felt hot. Her throat hurt. Her joints ached and she was sweating.

I can't believe this, Ashley thought. *I'm sick – on the most important day of my life!*

It was Wednesday morning, the day she was supposed to model her new school uniform at an all-school assembly.

If I don't model my new outfit, Ashley thought, *Mrs. Pritchard will go ahead with those horrible jumpers.*

The thought made her feel even *more* like throwing up than she already did.

"Aren't you getting up?" Phoebe asked.

"I'm sick," Ashley whispered hoarsely. "I can barely talk."

"Oh my gosh," Phoebe peered at Ashley in bed. "You look totally green."

"What am I going to do?" Ashley moaned. "The assembly . . . my uniform . . ." It hurt too much to talk.

"Don't worry about a thing," Phoebe announced. "I'll model it for you."

"You will?" Ashley's eyes were swollen and it hurt to lift her head. But she shot Phoebe a grateful half-smile. "Thanks. Great. It's in my closet . . ."

She couldn't talk any more. She couldn't even watch Phoebe get dressed.

She just rolled over and went back to sleep.

"Where is she?" Mary-Kate whispered.

"Who knows?" Campbell said. "I saw her carrying Ashley's outfit into the restroom in the hall. But she hasn't come out yet."

Mary-Kate turned to stare at the doorway, looking for Phoebe. The auditorium was packed with White Oak girls from all forms. First Form girls had to sit at the back. The oldest girls sat at the front.

Mrs. Pritchard was on the stage, at the microphone.

"So, as I said," Mrs. Pritchard went on, "we're very seriously considering school uniforms here at White Oak Academy. And one of our students, Ashley Burke, has graciously agreed to design an outfit that might serve as a uniform for everyone. But Ashley is sick today, I'm told. So her roommate, Phoebe Cahill, will be modelling it for us."

Mrs. Pritchard stared at the door. Waiting.

"Soon, I hope," she added, tapping her foot.

Finally the door swung open. Phoebe marched in. All the girls' heads turned to see the new uniform.

Mary-Kate gasped.

"Whoops!" she whispered to Campbell. "I don't think that's what Ashley had in mind!"

Phoebe was wearing the grey and white skirt Ashley had picked out. And the white sweater set.

But instead of the plain black tights Ashley had chosen, Phoebe had thrown on her own accessories.

She wore purple tights, an armful of plastic bangle bracelets, huge beaded earrings and a gold chain belt worn low around her hips. It jangled as she walked.

"Uh-oh," Campbell murmured.

"It's too colourful," Mary-Kate said. "Although on Phoebe, it's okay. She can pull it off."

Phoebe marched to the stage and paraded across it, towards Mrs. Pritchard.

"Oh, no," Mrs. Pritchard said, taking one look at her and shaking her head.

She let Phoebe parade back across the stage. Then she gave her a quick nod.

"Take your seat, please, Phoebe," Mrs. Pritchard ordered her. "Girls – I'm sorry. This seems to have been a waste of our time. I thought Ashley understood what the administration wanted. Something attractive and dignified. But I can see I've made a mistake by including student input."

"Uh, Mrs. Pritchard?" Mary-Kate tried to say, raising her hand from the back of the auditorium.

She had to explain what happened. That all those accessories weren't Ashley's idea!

But the Head either didn't see her or didn't want to. She went on. "So, girls, the administration will make the decision about uniforms *without* student input. We already have a very nice green and white proposal from an old girl. I'm sure we can all live with that. Thank you for coming."

"But Mrs. Pritchard," a girl from Sixth Form called, raising her hand. "Can't we at least—"

"I'm sorry – the discussion is closed!" the Head said sharply. "Now, everyone – please go to class."

*   *   *

"Ashley—I am *so* sorry," Phoebe said, bending close to Ashley's bed. "Really, I thought I was helping. I didn't mean to ruin your outfit. Can you ever forgive me?"

Ashley coughed and turned away. What could she say?

Not much, with her sore throat!

Besides, Phoebe had apologised five times. And brought chicken soup from the dining hall, since Ashley was too sick to go out.

She's such a good friend, Ashley thought. *Even if she is a flake!*

"I'm really sorry," Phoebe repeated again. "I just thought everyone would like the uniforms better if they knew they could add their own accessories. You know – personalise them."

"It's okay," Ashley croaked.

"Are you sure? Because I am *so* sorry! I promise I'll try to make it up to you somehow – when you're well."

When I'm well? I'll never be well, Ashley thought.

She felt so miserable, she didn't want to get out of bed ever again. And why should she?

After today she was going to be stuck with the ugliest school uniform she had ever seen in her life!

CHAPTER TEN

"Is she awake?" Mary-Kate asked, peeking into Ashley's room the next morning.

"I'm not sure," Phoebe whispered. "She's been moaning in her sleep."

"Gosh." Mary-Kate stared at her sister. Ashley had the covers pulled up over her head.

"Ashley?" she called softly. "Are you okay?"

Ashley lifted her head and peeked out.

"Hellllp," she moaned.

"Well, that answers that!" Mary-Kate said. "Your face is the same colour as our new school uniform – green!"

"I feel awful," Ashley whispered. "My throat is better, but I ache all over and . . ." She squinted.

58

"And everything looks funny. Your face is too bright. I see about ten different colours."

"That's my make-up!" Mary-Kate said, beaming. "Do you like it?"

"Are you kidding?" Ashley asked weakly. "I thought I was hallucinating!"

Wow, Mary-Kate thought. *She must really feel awful if she can't tell a great make-up job when she sees one!*

"Well, get some rest," she said. "I'll tell Miss Viola that you're staying in bed again today." Miss Viola was the housemother who lived in Porter House.

Mary-Kate scooted towards the door.

"Get my history assignments for me!" Ashley called after her.

"Okay," Mary-Kate called back.

Mary-Kate knocked on Miss Viola's door downstairs, but there was no answer. So she slipped a note under the door. Then she hurried to join Campbell at the shuttle bus stop. They were going to Harrington again today, for history.

Dylan Tunnell wasn't in Mary-Kate's class. But she always ran into him in the hall, before the bell.

"Do you think he'll notice me today?" Mary-Kate asked.

"How could he miss you?" Campbell said.

"You've got two different layers of eye shadow, mascara, heavy black eyeliner, two tones of lip liner, gloss, and a wedge of blusher that—"

"That perfectly accents my naturally sculpted cheeks," Mary-Kate explained. "You don't think it works?"

"It's a little over the top," Campbell said.

"I don't care. Dylan barely looked at me on Monday," Mary-Kate complained. "He's going to notice me today – for sure!"

"Here comes someone else who's going to notice you," Campbell warned. "The Head."

Mary-Kate turned around just in time to see Mrs. Pritchard marching towards her.

So what? Mary-Kate thought. *This wasn't like the Glitter Girls. Nothing outrageous or gothic. No green hair or anything. It was just a glamour look. Why should the Head care?*

Mary-Kate started to climb on to the bus.

"Mary-Kate?" Mrs. Pritchard called. "Hold on!"

Uh-oh. Mary-Kate knew that tone of voice. The Head didn't sound happy.

"I got a call from Miss Viola," Mrs. Pritchard began. "She saw you in the dining hall this morning, and claimed you were made up like a circus clown. I see she's right. That's much too

60

much make-up for White Oak. Please go straight back to Porter House and scrub it off."

"But I can't!" Mary-Kate cried. "I'll miss the shuttle bus! I'll miss my class!"

"That's too bad," Mrs. Pritchard said. She shook her head disapprovingly. "This is *exactly* why we need uniforms for classes."

Mary-Kate's face turned redder – if that was possible. It was so embarrassing to be yelled at in front of everyone. All the Second Form girls at the bus stop glared at her.

"Oh, wow, now we'll definitely get uniforms – thanks to *her*," one of the Second Form girls said.

"First Formers always ruin everything," another girl complained.

Great! Mary-Kate thought as she trudged back to her dorm. This day was turning out to be the pits! She was missing history class – which meant she'd probably get a bad grade on the next test.

And it's all for nothing, she realised. *Now I won't get to see Dylan till next week. And he'll never notice me without my make-up!*

CHAPTER ELEVEN

"Ashley – wake up!" Phoebe said, nudging her. "Are you alive?"

Ashley raised her head and squinted at her clock.

"What day is it?" Ashley asked.

"Friday," Phoebe said. "You've been in bed since Wednesday. Homecoming starts today. We've got to get moving. I've got a plan."

Ashley rubbed her eyes and swung her feet out of bed.

"Wow," she said. "I'm vertical!"

Phoebe laughed. "You look almost human, too. How do you feel?"

"I feel okay," Ashley said. "I think I'm over it – whatever it was."

"Good," Phoebe said, "because we don't have much time."

"For what?" Ashley asked.

"Just get dressed and come down to the lounge," Phoebe said. "You'll see."

Ashley hurried to join her friends downstairs. When she got there, Phoebe, Wendy, Elise, Samantha, Mary-Kate and Campbell were all waiting. The lounge looked great now. It was newly painted and decorated. Ashley's friends were kneeling on the floor, working on posters.

Ashley tilted her head sideways to read one.

UNIFORMITY KILLS CREATIVITY! the poster said.

"What's going on?" Ashley asked.

"I'm still not ready to give up and wear uniforms," Phoebe explained. "So we've organised a protest. We're making signs to carry. And Miss Viola said we could use these old curtains to make a huge banner."

"It'll say: NO UNIFORMS AT WHITE OAK!" Mary-Kate explained. "We'll hang it from the entrance to the dorm."

"Wow!" Ashley said, getting excited. "That's so cool!" She thought for a moment. "But I've got a better idea. Is it really okay if we ruin these old curtains?"

Wendy nodded. "We had to pull them out of the dumpster," she explained. "Miss Viola said it was fine."

"Excellent," Ashley said. Her eyes twinkled. "Has anybody seen *Gone with the Wind*?"

Phoebe shrugged. "Sure. Scarlett O'Hara makes a fancy ball gown out of the green velvet curtains in her house. So?"

"Come on, Ashley," Mary-Kate said, rolling her eyes. "You're *not* trying to get another dress out of this deal, are you?"

"No way. I'm thinking we should cut up the drapes – and make them into ugly green ponchos! They'll look sort of like the ugly green uniforms we're protesting," Ashley suggested. "We'll all wear them while we're marching in protest outside the administration building!"

"Wow," Phoebe said, nodding. "Brilliant idea. "That'll get everyone's attention."

"And maybe we really can change the trustees' minds," Wendy added. "I mean, they haven't voted yet. We *could* make a difference!"

"But we need girls from all forms," Ashley went on. "This can't just be a First Form protest."

Wendy agreed. "I know a few Third Form girls. I'll go and find them."

"And I know some Fifth Formers from softball," Campbell offered. "I could go and get them."

"Great!" Ashley said. "Mary-Kate, Elise and I will make the ponchos. Samantha – you and Phoebe just go into the dining hall and talk to people. Try to get girls to come back here for a poncho and a sign. The protest will start in one hour."

"Okay," Samantha headed out of the door.

"And bring me back a muffin!" Ashley called. "I'm starving. I haven't eaten yet."

"No muffins on Friday," Samantha reminded her.

"Oh. Right. Well, we'll have to protest *that* next month!"

An hour later the protest was in full swing. Twelve girls marched up and down outside Mrs. Pritchard's office. They all wore green ponchos and carried various signs that said:

UNIFORMS UNFAIR!

GREEN IS GROSS!

UNIFORMS IN SCHOOL – NOT COOL!

UNIFORMITY KILLS CREATIVITY!

Ashley's stomach was growling, but she didn't care. She was having too much fun!

The campus was crawling with White Oak graduates who had arrived for Homecoming weekend. Lots of women saw the signs and stopped to chat.

"What's this all about?" a pleasant woman asked Ashley.

"School uniforms," Ashley explained. "Mrs. Pritchard wants us to wear them. The Board of Trustees is voting on it this weekend."

"You're kidding!" the woman said. "Uniforms? At White Oak? I can't imagine that."

Ashley nodded.

The woman turned to a friend of hers. "Let's go and talk to Marcia about this," she said.

Yes! Ashley thought. *It's working!*

"UNIFORMITY KILLS CREATIVITY!" Ashley chanted, marching with her friends.

Two more women stopped to watch. Ashley saw them smiling.

"Remember when we protested about the war in Vietnam?" one of them said.

"It's good to see that these girls have the spirit to stand up for *something*," the second woman said. "Even if it's only the freedom to wear what they like."

"FREEDOM BEGINS WITH FASHION!" Ashley chanted.

Then Phoebe started a new chant.

"WE WON'T LEAVE OUR DORMS! NOT WEARING UNIFORMS!"

Ashley joined in. So did the other girls. Their voices grew louder and louder.

Pretty soon, a huge crowd of old pupils were standing around, watching.

Ashley pumped her sign in the air in rhythm with the chant. "WE WON'T . . . LEAVE OUR DORMS! NOT WEARING . . . UNIFORMS!" she chanted.

Whoops! How come she was the only person shouting that time?

Ashley whirled around and saw Mrs. Pritchard standing in front of the crowd. Her hands were planted on her hips.

She glared at Ashley and Mary-Kate.

"This is your idea, isn't it?" Mrs. Pritchard demanded sternly.

Ashley gulped. *My idea?* she thought. The ponchos were. But the protest had been Phoebe's.

Ashley didn't know what to say.

"I'll take your silence as a yes," Mrs. Pritchard snapped. "Don't you girls have any respect for other people's feelings?"

"Of course we do!" Ashley answered. "We aren't trying to hurt anyone's feelings. We're just . . ."

"Well, Mrs. Wainwright, who designed the new uniform, is in my office right now," the Head said, interrupting. "And I can tell you, she's not happy."

Oh, dear. Ashley hadn't thought about that.

"We'll apologise to her," Ashley said.

"I certainly hope you will," the Head said. "Just as soon as you put those horrible green ponchos in the trash."

"But Miss Viola gave us permission!" Phoebe blurted out.

The Head scowled even harder at that.

"I'm *sure* she didn't give you permission to make so much noise!" she scolded. "I want this protest to end right now – understand?"

Ashley and Mary-Kate nodded silently.

"And I'll deal with you two when Homecoming Weekend is over!" Mrs. Pritchard added.

Then she stormed off.

CHAPTER TWELVE

"Don't tell me you're not coming!" Mary-Kate said to her sister the next morning.

"To the mall?" Ashley said glumly. "What for? We'll be wearing nothing but green jumpers and white blouses for the rest of the year, and you know it."

Mary-Kate's face fell. She had been trying not to think about that. It was too depressing. And she had been trying not to think about how much trouble she and Ashley were in, either.

We'll probably be grounded for the rest of the term, Mary-Kate thought. This might be her last chance to leave campus!

"Please come with me," Mary-Kate begged. "You

can help me with my shopping spree. I need your advice. I'm trying to come up with a new look of my own."

"If you want your *own* look, how can I help?" Ashley asked.

Mary-Kate grinned. "I need you there to tell me which clothes *aren't* you!"

"Okay," Ashley gave in. "I'll come. But don't expect me to have any fun!"

Gosh, Mary-Kate thought. *Ashley's in such a bad mood. Maybe it won't be any fun – unless someone else comes along.*

She found Wendy and Phoebe hanging out in the lounge, and talked them into coming to the mall, too.

They took the shuttle bus at noon. But all four girls were having a hard time getting into the spirit of the thing.

"Where should we start?" Mary-Kate asked for suggestions.

Wendy glanced at the Chasm, one of their favourite stores. "How about there?" she pointed.

The girls headed towards the entrance. But the minute they got inside, something hit Mary-Kate in the eye.

Green!

There were bright green polo shirts, green jackets and green overalls all over the store.

"This reminds me too much of you-know-what," Mary-Kate said. "Let's try Portland's Palace instead."

But Portland's Palace wasn't much better. They had a lot of green clothes, too.

Green seemed to be the hot colour this season.

"Well, at least the new uniforms are a *colour* that's in style," Wendy mumbled, trying to be positive.

"Oh, right. By that logic, the maintenance man's uniform is to die for!" Ashley joked.

"I can't do it," Phoebe announced. "I just can't see myself wearing those uniforms. I'm thinking of transferring to another school if the board of trustees votes for them."

"You're kidding!" Ashley gasped. "You can't do that! I'd miss you too much!"

"Are you serious?" Mary-Kate asked. "You'd leave White Oak, just so you could wear vintage clothes?"

"Not just for vintage," Phoebe said. "I'd even be willing to wear ordinary khakis and sweaters and stuff. I'd go along with a dress code – but I can't go along with a jumper and white blouse that looks like someone's Home Ec. sewing project from the 1950s."

"Right," Mary-Kate said. "A dress code. That would be fair."

"Maybe that's what we should have marched for. We should have campaigned for that on our protest signs," Wendy said. "Too late now."

Too late? No, it isn't, Mary-Kate thought. *Not yet. Not until the board votes!*

She grabbed Wendy by her arm. "Listen. What if we come up with a dress code that the board would approve? I could use my shopping spree money to buy one perfect outfit for each of us. They'd all be different – but they'd all be something Mrs. Pritchard could stand."

"What good will that do?" Phoebe asked.

"We could model them for the board of trustees!" Mary-Kate exclaimed. "To convince them to vote for a dress code instead of uniforms. Would your mom let us do that?"

"I'm not sure." Wendy thought a bit. "I've been begging my mom to tell me how she's going to vote on the uniforms – and she won't."

"You mean she's *against* us?" Ashley cried.

"I *hope* not," Wendy said. "I think she just doesn't want me telling everyone if she votes against Mrs. Pritchard's plan."

"Call her," Mary-Kate pleaded. "Find out if she'll

talk the board into letting us make a presentation."

Wendy nodded, and the girls hurried to a pay phone. Wendy dialled her mother's mobile phone number. She talked for a few minutes and then gave Mary-Kate the thumbs-up.

"We're on!" Wendy announced. "We can have fifteen minutes tomorrow to model our outfits before the board votes."

"Yes!" Mary-Kate said, shooting her fist into the air.

"Let's shop!" Ashley said, looking happy for the first time all day.

It took four hours to find outfits for all of them. But when they were done, all four girls were psyched. They had all picked out clothes that were conservative enough to please the adults at school – but cool enough so they really wanted to wear them.

Mary-Kate bought a pair of black velvet trousers, black suede sneakers and a white hooded sweater.

Ashley chose a dressier look – a heather grey skirt with a matching grey sweater trimmed in beads.

"I love my outfit!" Wendy said, giving Mary-Kate a hug as they waited for the shuttle bus back to school.

Wendy had chosen a ski sweater knitted in lots of colourful little patterns. It looked fabulous with plain brown corduroys and new hiking boots.

"Me, too," Phoebe said. "Thanks for helping me find something so . . . so retro!"

Phoebe's outfit was the most unusual. It was a white hooded dress with a bulky zipper down the front. It was sort of a cross between a British mod look and sixties disco. It was cool – but not outrageous. And it wasn't too-too short.

Mary-Kate thought Mrs. Pritchard would approve.

"I'm psyched," Ashley whispered to her sister. "I think this plan might actually work! But you know what the problem is."

Mary-Kate nodded. "Phoebe," she whispered. "Her dress is fine . . ."

"Right," Ashley agreed. "But the big problem is: How are we going to keep her from accessorising it?"

CHAPTER THIRTEEN

Ashley leaped out of bed early on Sunday morning. This was it – the big day. The day that would decide how she would look for the rest of the school year.

Like a real girl? Or a munchkin?

Phoebe was already up and dressed.

"How do I look?" Phoebe asked, modelling her new dress in front of their mirror.

Ashley gulped. "Great!" she said. "Except . . ."

"You don't like the boots," Phoebe guessed quickly.

Ashley shook her head. Phoebe was wearing knee-high white patent-leather boots.

"They go with the dress perfectly," Ashley admitted. "But they make the whole thing too . . ."

"Too vintage? Too out there? Too weird?" Phoebe asked.

"All three," Ashley agreed.

Phoebe sighed and changed into a pair of flat black shoes. Ashley could tell she was disappointed.

"Just stay focused on our goal," Ashley reminded her. "No green uniforms!"

Mary-Kate popped her head into Ashley's room.

"Hi," she said nervously. "How do I look?"

"Great," Ashley said. "It's a whole new you. I could tell you apart from *me* any day!"

"Very funny," Mary-Kate said. "Listen, has anyone seen Wendy?"

"Not yet," Ashley answered. "Why?"

"She's not in her room," Mary-Kate explained. "And I don't know what time the board meeting is!"

"Oh my gosh," Ashley said. "Do you think they're meeting already? And we're late?"

"I don't know. We'd better run over there and find out!" Mary-Kate replied.

"You go," Ashley said. "If she's there, come back and tell us. Otherwise, Phoebe and I will go and find Wendy – somehow."

Mary-Kate nodded and dashed out of the dorm.

Ashley grabbed her jacket. Then she took one last

look at Phoebe. Something big and paisley was hanging around Phoebe's neck.

"Lose the scarf," she ordered her roommate.

Phoebe sighed. "It's just so hard to wear all brand-new clothes!" she complained.

Ashley and Phoebe hurried out of Porter House and glanced around. No sign of Wendy anywhere.

But women of all ages were crisscrossing the campus, enjoying their visit back to White Oak.

"Let's check the dining hall," Phoebe suggested. "Maybe she's having breakfast."

No luck. Wendy wasn't there.

"How about the student centre?" Ashley said.

Nope. Wendy wasn't in the student centre either.

They ran to the gym, the computer centre, and then back to the dorm. Wendy wasn't anywhere.

"Look – there's Mrs. Wainwright," Ashley said.

Ashley felt a lump in her throat. She still felt terrible about hurting Mrs. Wainwright's feelings.

"Wait here. I'm going to talk to her," Ashley said. She hurried across the green to catch up with the older woman.

"Mrs. Wainwright?" she called.

"Yes?" The old pupil turned and frowned at her.

"I just wanted to tell you how sorry I am if we hurt your feelings," Ashley said. "With our protest."

Mrs. Wainwright didn't say a word. She just looked at Ashley.

"We weren't making fun of your design," Ashley went on. "Or we didn't mean to anyway. We were protesting the idea of wearing *any* uniforms. No matter who designed them – or what colour they are."

That's the truth, Ashley thought. *At least the last part is.*

"Well, thank you," Mrs. Wainwright said, cracking a small smile. "I appreciate your courtesy in coming up to me."

Ashley glanced at her watch. She still hadn't found Wendy, and the board meeting could be starting any minute!

"Excuse me," she said to Mrs. Wainwright. "I've got to go. I'm looking for a friend."

"Good luck," Mrs. Wainwright called.

Ashley hurried over to Phoebe. "I'll check Wendy's room again. Be right back."

She trudged up the two flights of stairs. Wendy's room was at the top – and her door was standing open.

Bingo! Ashley thought.

Until she peered inside.

"Oh, hello," said a young woman with a baby in

her arms. "Is this your room? Sorry for barging in, but I used to live here fifteen years ago."

"That's fine – I mean, I guess," Ashley said. "It's not my room. Have you seen Wendy – the girl who lives here? She has long brown hair. And she's wearing a colourful ski sweater with brown cords . . . or at least she should be . . ."

"Sorry," the woman said. "No one's been here but me."

"Well, if you see her, would you tell her to meet me at the main building?" Ashley asked before dashing out of the room.

Phoebe and Ashley ran all the way across campus. They were out of breath by the time they got to the Head's office. Mary-Kate was tapping her foot, waiting outside.

"Where have you been?" she asked Ashley. "Four of the board members are already in there!"

"We can't find Wendy," Phoebe explained. She scanned the campus desperately. "What are we going to do?"

Just then a car pulled into the parking lot. Wendy jumped out and ran towards them.

"Hi!" she called. "Ready?"

"Yes!" Ashley answered. "We've been ready all morning. Where have *you* been?"

"I stayed with my mom last night in a motel," Wendy answered.

Wendy's mother, Mrs. Linden, came up the walk with a friendly smile on her face.

"All right, girls," she said. "Let's go inside. This is your big moment."

Ashley's stomach did a little flip-flop. A lot was riding on this.

They followed Mrs. Linden into a small room next to the big conference room. Mrs. Pritchard was waiting there.

"Hello, girls," she welcomed them. "We'll be ready for you in the conference room in just a moment. I'm going to explain the idea of the dress code to the other board members. Then I'll bring you in. Please put on these name tags, so that the board members can call you by name if they have any questions."

"Name tags?" Ashley cried. "But – that won't look good on our outfits!"

"Shh!" Mary-Kate shushed Ashley. "Let's just do what she asks. And keep your fingers crossed!"

A few minutes later Ashley and her friends stood in front of the board.

"Would you like to make your case?" Mrs. Linden said to Ashley.

Yikes! Ashley thought. She didn't realise she would have to make a speech!

She took a deep breath and began. "We just think we should be able to have a dress code," she said. "Instead of school uniforms. I mean, uniforms are so . . ."

What was the word?

"So *uniform*," Phoebe chimed in. "It makes us all feel like we're supposed to be alike. But we're not. We're all different people. And we want a chance to express our differences in the way we dress."

"Right," Ashley picked up the ball again. "But we understand that school should be a place where students show respect for teachers. And that the classroom is a place to work. So I guess the clothes we wear to class should be different from our just-hanging-out clothes, right? That's where the dress code comes in."

She stopped and glanced around the room.

How are we doing? Ashley wondered.

The women seemed to be smiling. Most of them, anyway. But the Head didn't look happy at all. Her face was set like stone.

"Our rules would be no T-shirts, no sweatshirts and no skirts above a certain length for class," Ashley explained.

"And no navels showing, no spaghetti straps, and no jeans or very baggy trousers," Mary-Kate added.

"And no pyjamas," Phoebe chimed in. "Except for sleeping, of course."

Mrs. Linden peered at Phoebe's name tag. "Phoebe, are you the girl who started the protest?" she asked.

Phoebe shot Ashley a worried glance.

"Uh, we started it together," Ashley answered. "It was Phoebe's idea, but we all joined in."

Mrs. Linden nodded and turned to the woman beside her. "Remember our Save the Whales march, Rosa?" she asked.

Rosa smiled. "We were so passionate in those days!"

"And I remember signing a petition," someone else said. "Remember, Sherry? We demanded that the headmistress – it was Mrs. Bonniker at the time – let us add two chapters to the history text. We wanted it to include the civil rights marches."

"Those were the good old days!" Sherry replied.

She shot Ashley an approving smile.

"Okay, okay, enough reminiscing," Mrs. Linden said. "Let's get down to business. Who likes the green uniforms that Mrs. Wainwright designed?"

"Before you answer, let me say something," Mrs. Pritchard jumped in. "We certainly don't have to use Claudia's design. But that doesn't mean we should abandon school uniforms entirely. I'm sure I could come up with a design myself."

"That's true, I suppose," Rosa agreed.

Mrs. Linden and the other board members exchanged glances. They didn't seem to want to say anything more – not in front of the girls.

"Wendy, could you and the others please wait outside?" Mrs. Linden asked. "I think we're ready to vote. But we want to do it in private."

"Sure," Wendy answered.

Ashley's heart sank as she followed her friends out into the hall.

"What do you think?" Mary-Kate asked Wendy. "Will your mom vote against Mrs. Pritchard?"

"I think they want to keep the Head happy," Wendy answered.

"Which means we're going to be dressed like leprechauns on St. Patrick's Day," Ashley said. "For the rest of our lives!"

CHAPTER FOURTEEN

"How long does it take to vote?" Phoebe wondered, staring at the clock in the hall.

Mary-Kate paced back and forth. They'd been waiting for half an hour already. But it seemed like longer.

"Listen," Wendy said, edging towards the door. "I think I heard someone laugh."

"Is that a good sign?" Mary-Kate asked.

Wendy shrugged. "Beats me."

Phoebe bit one of her fingernails. "What's taking so long?" she mumbled again.

Who knows? Mary-Kate thought. She stared hard at the door to the conference room.

"I'm really going to transfer to another school,"

Phoebe said quietly. "I mean, if they make us wear uniforms. I can't stay here."

"Take me with you!" Ashley joked.

Don't look at the clock again, Mary-Kate told herself. *It's just making you more nervous!*

But she couldn't help it.

"They've been in there forty-five minutes!" Mary-Kate moaned.

"It must mean they're arguing," Wendy said. "My mom said it always takes a long time to vote when they don't agree."

"But which side is winning?" Phoebe wondered out loud.

Just then the door swung open.

"Girls?" Mrs. Pritchard said. "Could you come inside?"

Mary-Kate held her breath. They all walked into the conference room.

She checked out the faces of the board members. They were smiling.

"Congratulations," Mrs. Pritchard said. "You've won!"

"What?" Mary-Kate gasped. She couldn't believe it.

"We've won!" Ashley screamed, jumping up and down.

Mrs. Pritchard smiled broadly. "You girls came up with a reasonable plan," she said. "I must say the board and I are proud of you. We've decided to adopt your ideas. The board voted in favour of a dress code – but no uniforms."

"Yes!" Wendy said.

Mrs. Pritchard laughed. "All right. We just wanted to thank you in person."

"Thank you, girls," Mrs. Linden said. "You've helped us quite a bit."

"And Ashley," Mrs. Pritchard said softly. "Thank you for speaking to Mrs. Wainwright earlier today. I ran into her, and she told me about your apology. That helped us quite a bit, too."

Ashley beamed.

Mary-Kate waited until they were back outside to hug her sister.

"We won!" she cheered. "I can't believe it. Thank you – all of you!"

"No – thank *you*," Phoebe said. "Without your shopping spree, this never would have happened!"

"I can't wait to tell everyone," Ashley announced. Ashley, Phoebe and Wendy started down the steps to the centre of campus.

"Wait!" Mary-Kate called. She motioned her sister to come back.

"What?" Ashley and the other girls returned.

"Look," Mary-Kate pointed to a group of people who were walking slowly towards them. "It's Dylan Tunnell! What's he doing here?"

"It looks like he's with his mom," Ashley said. "She must be a White Oak old girl, and he's visiting campus with her."

"What should I do?" Mary-Kate asked. "He's coming this way!"

"Just be calm," Ashley said. "Act cool. Let's not stand here gawking. We'll walk towards them."

Mary-Kate tossed her hair over her shoulders. She and her friends walked right up to Dylan and his mom.

"Hey, Mary-Kate," he said, looking her right in the eye. "Cool sweater."

Yes! Mary-Kate thought. *He recognised me!*

"He got your name right!" Ashley said, leaning in close to whisper. "And he likes your sweater!"

Mary-Kate did a double take.

"No wonder!" she whispered to Ashley, turning away so Dylan wouldn't hear. "He's wearing the same thing!"

Mary-Kate grinned and moved a little closer to Dylan.

"Congratulations," she said to him. "You got my name right this time. How did you know I'm Mary-Kate, and not Ashley?"

"Duh," he said, giving her a strange look. "It was easy."

"It was?" Mary-Kate was still confused.

"Sure," Dylan answered with a grin. "You're wearing a name tag!"

WELCOME BACK, SQUIRRELS!
by Phoebe Cahill

Attention all White Oakers! Hide your cashews! Put your peanuts in a safe! Because next weekend, our campus will be crawling with hundreds of squirrels!

That's right – it's Homecoming Weekend! And we all know what that means. White Oak old girls, who proudly call themselves the White Oak Squirrels, will be coming back for a three-day visit. It's their chance to talk over old times and snoop around in their old dorm rooms. (So get busy cleaning under your beds!)

Let's all show them that this school is still the same

great place that it was 100 years ago when it was founded. (They'd have to be *nuts* to think it isn't!)

GLAM GAB
Freedom of Dress
Opinion by Phoebe

A terrible injustice is about to happen at White Oak. Our freedom of expression is being yanked away – and we'll all be left looking like rows of miniature robots!

Why? Because school uniforms are on their way!

What's next? Brainwashing? Freedom to dress the way we want is very important to us. How else can we show that we're individuals? Our clothes express our personalities. They tell the world that we're either bold or shy . . . creative or creepy . . . outgoing or outrageous. If we can't choose what to wear each day, it's sort of like not being allowed to decide what kind of person we want to be!

It's certainly not what I expected when I signed up for a White Oak education. And I doubt it's what my classmates expected, either. But does White Oak care about our feelings? I guess we'll all have to wait and see!

First Form for Uniforms
Opinion by Ashley

Fashion expert Ashley Burke

What's all the uproar about wearing school uniforms? I, for one, think the idea has some definite pluses and should be given serious consideration.

For one thing, have you ever thought about how much we compete over fashion? Sure, it's fun to wear the coolest new outfits to class – especially when we go over to Harrington! But some people, believe it or not,

have a hard time keeping up with the fashion trends. Wearing school uniforms would help them by cutting down on the hot-and-heavy competition to always be well dressed.

Another good thing about uniforms is that they cost less. Think about the savings! The people who can't afford expensive clothes would feel better, too. Everyone would look the same, which means everyone would feel equal.

Last but not least, wearing school uniforms shows our teachers that we respect the classroom. It shows that we know what we're there for – to work.

So let's all give school uniforms a second thought – and a chance. Uniforms might not be the hippest things in the world, but they aren't the *end* of the world either.

THE GET-REAL GIRL

Dear Get-Real Girl,
The guy I'm crushing on has been flirting with my roommate. She *knows* how much I like him, but she's still flirting back! I can't believe she'd betray me like this. What am I supposed to do – spell it out for her? Tell her he's mine – and to keep her grubby hands off?

Signed,
Mad and Miserable

Dear Mad and Miserable,
Are you kidding? You think this guy is your own

personal property just because you've been crushing on him for a few weeks? Get real! If he's yours, here's a news flash for you: someone forgot to tell him! Because it sounds like he's a lot more interested in your *roomie* than in you!

Instead of whining about it, why not put yourself in your roomie's shoes? (And

if they're your size, you've probably done that already!) Ask yourself: what would you do if some cutie flirted with *you* – and your roommate liked him, too? Would you ignore him – just to give her a better chance?

Probably not. So don't expect her to be more self-sacrificing than you are.

Instead, find someone else to concentrate on.

Signed,
Get-Real Girl

Dear Get-Real Girl,
My best friend is the *best*. There's only one prob-

lem – she constantly steals my food. At breakfast, she begs for my muffin. At lunch, she picks pepperonis off my pizza. And at dinner tonight, she ate all the icing on my cupcake when I wasn't looking! How can I stop her?

Signed,
Hungry

Dear Hungry,
It sounds to me like it's time for a little talk. Point out to your friend that pepperonis are your favourite part of the pizza, too – and you don't feel like giving them away! But if the problem continues, my advice

is to fight fire with fire – or in this case, muffins with muffins. Start begging for

hers every morning. Then grab her milkshake at lunch. She'll get the idea soon enough. (And if you manage to get her fudge pie away from her at dinner, save it for me! It's my fave!)

Signed,
Get-Real Girl

THE FIRST FORM BUZZ
by Dana Woletsky

What a week it's been! Monday started out with a bang when EVH and company wore satin nightgowns to bio class in protest. (Protesting *what*? That none of the guys ever notice them?) But did anyone hear the *real* dish? Apparently BR was cheating. She actually had

blue jeans on underneath her jams! Talk about being a chicken! Or should I say "cow"? After all, it *is* the first syllable of *coward*!

And speaking of cowards, why is it that a certain First Form twin with the initials MKB can't bring herself to let DT know how much she likes him? All those trips to the pencil sharpener in bio are just not working, MKB! Try sharpening your flirting skills instead!

But the really hot rumour is that someone's been sneaking out of Porter House every night – to make a doughnut run into town and back! I'm not naming names – but who else, other than CW, can jog two miles without breaking a sweat? Maybe she ought to share those goodies with some of the Phipps Dormers, if she doesn't want to read her name in the newspaper next week!

Well, that's about it for the buzz. But remember my motto: if you want the scoop, you just gotta snoop!
The Buzz Girl

HOOP-LA!
White Oak Swishes to Victory Over Marylebone
by Mary-Kate Burke

The night was cool, but the White Oak Squirrels were

Sports pro Mary-Kate Burke

definitely hot last Saturday when they won their first game of the basketball season against Marylebone School. Everyone said it was a game to remember – and I, for one, will never forget it!

The excitement started when our captain Campbell Smith scored a three-pointer during the first two minutes of the game. Then we squirrelled away eight more points. Marylebone Captain Danica Morris, who is nicknamed "Tall Girl", practically flipped when yours truly shot a three-pointer in the last minute of the game.

Before leaving the floor, the Marylebone Monsters congratulated us. "Tall Girl" was heard to make some kind of "short" joke about one of our players – I'm not saying who. But Campbell Smith had the final word. She shot back, "Hey, we didn't come up short where it counts – in the final score!" Right on, Roomie! You tell 'em!

UPCOMING CALENDAR – AUTUMN/ WINTER

It's time to go trick-or-treating at the faculty houses on Saturday, October 28. Scariest make-up wins the

White Oak Haunters prize. (Don't worry – the teachers aren't allowed to enter!)

Calling all superstars! Don't forget that it's all about do-re-*me* at the auditions for the annual musical. (What musical? It's a surprise!) Get ready to sing your heart out on Friday, November 3, at 4:00 p.m. in the auditorium. Good luck to all!

Just hear those sleigh bells ring-a-ling! All White Oak girls and Harrington guys are invited to the Holiday Sleigh Ride on Sunday, December 10! Talk about horsing around!

Freaked about your French exam? Bogged down in bio? Miserable about maths? No sweat – just sign up for a tutor in the computer centre and get help with end-of-term exams. Study on!

Hurry home for the holidays – but don't forget to come back in time for the

White Oak/Harrington Winter Festival the weekend of January 29/30. Bring your skis, skates and snowboards. Let it snow, let it snow, let it snow!

It's All in the Stars
Autumn/Winter Horoscopes

Scorpio:
(Oct. 23–Nov. 21)

Don't look now, but the stars are lined up to shine on you this month. All you have to do is step outside and greet the world with that I'm-ready-for-anything smile – and you'll be on your way to making big things happen. Just remember to back up your smile with a nothing-can-stop-me attitude. And nothing will!

Sagittarius:
(Nov. 22–Dec. 21)

Your sign is the archer – and you know what that means. You're a hunter at heart – willing to go after whatever you want. A new guy? No problem for you. You'll just march right up and talk to him! Need more friends? You'll throw a party! (But don't forget to clean up afterwards. Otherwise, someone in your family will be hunting for *you*!)

Capricorn:
(Dec. 22–Jan. 19)

Look out, Capricorn. Everyone knows you like to climb every mountain – just be careful you don't fall off! So kick back. Don't take on too many after-school projects at once. And leave a little time in your busy schedule for the things that really count – like your friends.

PSST! Take a sneak peek at

Bye-Bye Boyfriend

"Okay, let's take it from the top," Mr. Boulderblatt called out during the dress rehearsal of *Bye Bye Birdie*. "Let's have the 'One Last Kiss' number." He nodded at Jeremy to say his line.

Jeremy crossed his arms and hunched up his shoulders. "And now a treat for all you youngsters," Jeremy announced. "Let's hear it for – Conrad Birdie!"

Ross Lambert turned to Mary-Kate, who was playing Birdie's biggest fan. Swinging his hips and strumming his guitar, Ross began to sing, "One Last Kiss".

Mary-Kate tried to appear starry-eyed. She knew that she was supposed to act thrilled that "Conrad Birdie" was about to kiss her. But she was still nervous.

Mary-Kate held her breath as Ross leaned over. But just as he began to pucker up—

"Stop!" Ashley shouted.

Mary-Kate froze.

"I have to take Kim's measurements right now!" Ashley said as she ran to Mary-Kate with a measuring tape.

"Now?" Mr. Boulderblatt cried. "During a dress rehearsal?"

"Her jacket might be too tight!" Ashley told Boulderblatt. She swung the measuring tape like a lasso around Mary-Kate.

"Ashley," Mr. Boulderblatt growled. "Go back to the costume room. Pleeeeease?"

"Okay," Ashley said, taking back the measuring tape. "No problem."

Mary-Kate noticed that Ashley's eyes were on Ross as she walked away with Phoebe.

Wait a minute, Mary-Kate thought. *Ashley said she didn't care about the kiss – even though Ross is almost her boyfriend. So what's up?*

"Now, let's try this again," Mr. Boulderblatt groaned. "Conrad is about to kiss Kim. Take it from the pucker."

Here goes, Mary-Kate thought as Ross leaned over to kiss her. *Should I keep my eyes open or closed? Should I move closer to him or do I wait until he moves closer to me? Did I remember to take my gum out?*

But just as Ross's and Mary-Kate's lips were about to meet—

WHIIIIIIRRRRRRRRRRRR!!!!

Mary-Kate and Ross clapped their hands over their ears.

"It's that blasted sewing machine!" Mr. Boulderblatt cried, throwing his script on the floor.

Everyone turned towards the costume room. Ashley slowly poked her head out of the door and smiled. "Sorry," she squeaked.

Mary-Kate groaned with everyone else. Ashley had interrupted the kissing scene again!

I guess she does care if I kiss Ross, Mary-Kate thought. *She cares a lot!*

mary-kateandashley

TWO of a kind ™

Coming soon – can you collect them all?

HarperCollins*Entertainment*

 PARACHUTE PRESS

DUALSTAR PUBLICATIONS

AOL mary-kateandashley.com
AOL Keyword: mary-kateandashley

TM & © 2002 Dualstar Entertainment Group, LLC.

mary-kateandashley

Meet Chloe and Riley Carlson.

So much to do...

so little time

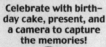

Mary-Kate and Ashley's latest exciting movie adventure

Available to own on video and DVD 29th July 2002

mary-kateandashley.com
AOL Keyword: mary-kateandashley

It's What YOU Watch!

DUALSTAR VIDEO

Mary-Kate and Ashley Sweet 16

PlayStation 2 · GAME BOY ADVANCE · GAMECUBE

DUALSTAR INTERACTIVE

Games for Girls

mary-kateandashley.com
AOL Keyword: mary-kateandashley

CLUB Acclaim

Real Books or Real Girls

It's What YOU Read

b the 1st 2 kno
mary-kateandashley

REGISTER 4 THE HARPERCOLLINS AND MK&ASH TEXT CLUB AND KEEP UP2 D8 WITH THE L8EST MK&ASH BOOK NEWS AND MORE.

SIMPLY TEXT TOK, FOLLOWED BY YOUR GENDER (M/F), DATE OF BIRTH (DD/MM/YY) AND POSTCODE TO: 07786277301.

SO, IF YOU ARE A GIRL BORN ON THE 12TH MARCH 1986 AND LIVE IN THE POSTCODE DISTRICT RG19 YOUR MESSAGE WOULD LOOK LIKE THIS: TOKF120386RG19.

IF YOU ARE UNDER 14 YEARS WE WILL NEED YOUR PARENTS' OR GUARDIANS' PERMISSION FOR US TO CONTACT YOU. PLEASE ADD THE LETTER 'G' TO THE END OF YOUR MESSAGE TO SHOW YOU HAVE YOUR PARENTS' CONSENT. LIKE THIS: TOKF120386RG19G.

HarperCollins*Entertainment*

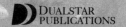

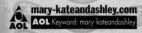

mary-kateandashley.com
AOL Keyword: mary-kateandashley

Order Form

To order direct from the publishers, just make a list of the titles you want and fill in the form below:

Name ....

Address ....

....

....

Send to: Dept 6, HarperCollins Publishers Ltd, Westerhill Road, Bishopbriggs, Glasgow G64 2QT.

Please enclose a cheque or postal order to the value of the cover price, plus:

UK & BFPO: Add £1.00 for the first book, and 25p per copy for each additional book ordered.

Overseas and Eire: Add £2.95 service charge. Books will be sent by surface mail but quotes for airmail despatch will be given on request.

A 24-hour telephone ordering service is available to holders of Visa, MasterCard, Amex or Switch cards on 0141- 772 2281.

An imprint of HarperCollins*Publishers*